Turnip Tom and Big Fat Rosie
Mary Calvert

Big Fat Rosie was the biggest, fattest person there ever was. Everything she did was done enormously. Her husband was a farmer called Turnip Tom, and in the farmhouse all the doors were extra-wide so that Big Fat Rosie could move around. Big Fat Rosie had to sleep in an extra-wide bed and sit on an extra-wide chair. She was very greedy indeed, and her favourite food was cream buns.

Here are seven hilarious stories about this new character, whose arrival on *Listen with Mother* has been received with enormous enthusiasm. Now young listeners can laugh at Big Fat Rosie whenever they wish, and storyteller and listener alike will enjoy Roger Smith's amusing illustrations.

D1437896

Turnip Tom and

Mary Calvert

illustrated by Roger Smith

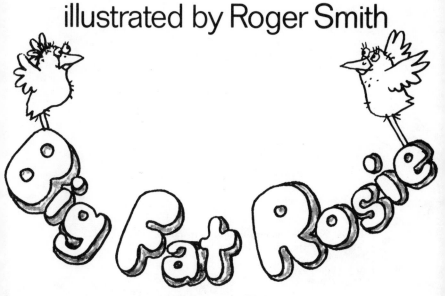

Big Fat Rosie

British Broadcasting Corporation

For James and Harry Calvert

Published by the British Broadcasting Corporation,
35 Marylebone High Street, London W1M 4AA
ISBN 0 563 12368 0
First published 1972
© Mary Calvert 1972

Printed in England by John Blackburn Ltd, Leeds

Before we begin

Big Fat Rosie is a recent arrival on the *Listen with Mother* scene. Her appeal is in her huge childishness: her tears, her giggle, her passion for cream buns. These stories will be enjoyed by children older than five, but younger children respond to Rosie's simplicity and Mary Calvert's marvellous sound effects. These need to be larger than life when read aloud, and mothers could well benefit from a little practice in the harder sounds, such as "ompa chompah" the noise of Rosie's eating, or the groaning "eee-aah-eee-err" of the pump in the yard. Fathers are often found to be experts at cows moo-ing and ponies trotting. As children like making the sounds too, we hope the book will lead to some interesting family performances and the discovery of unexpected talents.

Jenyth Worsley, Producer

Are you sitting comfortably? Then I'll begin

The Biggest Cream Bun in the World

BIG Fat Rosie was the biggest, fattest person there ever was.

She was bigger than a barrel.

She was plumper than a pudding.

She was rounder than a rubber ball.

And almost as heavy as a medium-sized hippopotamus.

And Big Fat Rosie was very, very wide. She was so wide that:

She had to sit on an extra-wide chair.

She had to sleep in an extra-wide bed.

She had to eat with an extra-wide spoon.

And all the doors in her house were extra-extra wide, so that she could move from room to room without getting stuck.

Everything that Big Fat Rosie did was done enormously. When she ate (with her extra-wide spoon), she made a noise like this

7

When she slept (in her extra-wide bed), she snored like this

and all the walls quivered.

When she cried, like this

such huge tears fell from her eyes that everything around her became soaking wet.

Big Fat Rosie was a farmer's wife, and her husband was called Turnip Tom. While Rosie looked after the house, Turnip Tom managed everything around the farm. He had pigs and cows and ducks and chickens and he grew wheat, cabbages, potatoes and, of course, turnips. Turnip Tom was very good to Big Fat Rosie and bought her plenty of nice things to eat. This made Big Fat Rosie happy, because she was very greedy indeed – and her favourite food was cream buns.

One day, when Turnip Tom was out working in the fields, Big Fat Rosie thought she would give him a surprise. She would make a great big cream bun and they could eat it together for their tea. She giggled happily, like this

and made a list of all the things she would need:
flour, eggs, milk, butter, sugar and cream.

There were big bags of flour and sugar in the
larder, but the other ingredients would have to be
collected from the farm.

Big Fat Rosie put on her rubber farm boots and
went first to the cowshed, where Old Harry, the
farm-boy, was putting hay in the cows' manger.
Outside, the cows made hungry, waiting noises,
like this

"Hallo Harry," said Big Fat Rosie. "Please may I have some milk and some butter and some cream? I'm going to make the biggest cream bun in the world."

"Arr," said Harry, scratching his head. "When a bun's big as that, there'll be some as gets fat."

"Yes," agreed Rosie, laughing cosily, "me." (Because, of course, she was already as fat as a couple of eiderdowns.)

Harry went into the dairy and came out with a can of milk, a bowl of butter and a jug of cream. Big Fat Rosie thanked him and trotted off towards the henhouse to look for some eggs.

When the hens saw her, they made a fearful racket, like this

and flapped about her feet.

"No, no!" cried Big Fat Rosie. "It isn't tea-time yet. I've come to fetch some eggs." She went over to the nesting boxes and looked inside. There were ten beautiful speckly-brown eggs, some of them still warm. She put them in her apron pocket and walked carefully back to the farmhouse, trying not to bump them with her knees. "Hee hee!" she thought. "Now I can make the biggest cream bun in the world!"

When the mixture was ready in the bowl, Big Fat Rosie stirred it with her wooden spoon, like this

and licked her lips. She tasted the mixture twenty-six times, just to be sure it was right, and added a few spoonfuls of yeast. Yeast would make the bun rise splendidly, like a loaf of bread. Turnip Tom *would* be pleased.

Big Fat Rosie bent down to light the oven. It made a noise like this

and she poured the bun mixture on to the biggest baking tray she could find. When she had placed it in the oven, she sat in her very wide rocking chair and hummed a little happy tune as she rocked, like this

And then she fell asleep.

In the oven, the bun was rising higher and higher. In the chair, Rosie was snoring louder and louder, like this

The whole kitchen was shaking with the noise – until suddenly the oven door burst open with a bang. Big Fat Rosie woke up, rubbed her eyes and looked around her. What on earth was that peculiar sound? It went like this

It was the bun! It was pouring out of the oven! Over the floor it crept steadily, blobbing and bubbling, slopping and slurping. It looked as though it would never stop. But Big Fat Rosie was not going to be beaten by a bun. She knew she could never sweep it up – but she could eat it. It was almost time for tea, anyway. She grabbed the nearest piece and began to eat very fast, like this

But the bun kept on coming. It was rising up the table legs and Big Fat Rosie had to eat even faster, like this

She wished she had never put all that yeast in the mixture.

Then the bun began to creep over the window sill and out into the garden. Turnip Tom, coming home from the fields, called out to Harry.

"Come quick! There's a bun climbing out of the window!"

"Dearie me," said Harry and hurried with him to the kitchen. There they found Big Fat Rosie knee deep in bun, eating more and more slowly, like this

"Omp," she mumbled, almost in tears. "It was going – omp – to be the biggest chomp bomp in the womp."

"Never mind," said Turnip Tom, who always knew exactly what to do, "Harry and I can take it away in a barrow."

"Arr," said Harry.

They fetched their shovels and a wheelbarrow and began to scrape the cream bun off the walls. Harry switched off the oven and the rest of the dough began to sink. Finally, it stopped. Turnip Tom gave a great big sigh of relief, like this

and stood looking thoughtfully at the barrowload of bun. "We could bury it in the garden," he suggested.

Harry said: "When a bun gets too big, remember the pig."

So they gave the bun to Alexander, who was always hungry, and he grunted happily, like this

as if to say "Thank you very much."

But Big Fat Rosie thought he was saying "What a rotten cook" and decided she would make another biggest cream bun in the world tomorrow, just to show him. And this time it would be even bigger.

Big Fat Rosie Saves the Day

IT was a very hot summer. Turnip Tom heard on
the radio that there hadn't been such a dry
summer for twenty years. He looked out at the
parched fields and the shimmery blue sky and he
sighed, like this

and wiped his forehead with a spotted handkerchief. All the seeds he had planted in the spring would die soon if it didn't rain. Already the little green shoots were turning yellow and hanging their heads. In the farmyard, things weren't much better. Maisie, the Guernsey cow, put her head over the fence and mooed pathetically, like this

and three of the lambs were bleating, one after another, like this

Old Alexander the pig merely lay on his pink side in the straw, letting out cross grunts, like this

19

If only the river hadn't dried up, thought Turnip Tom, he could fetch them all some water. But even the pump in the yard was making groaning noises, like this

eee-aah
"eee eer"

and the taps in the house would give only a tiny trickle of water – hardly enough to fill an egg cup.

Turnip Tom thought hard. Where could he find some water? There was very little to be had in the village. Although a big tanker came every day with drinking water for the villagers, they were only allowed half a bucketful each. That was not enough for all Turnip Tom's animals and all the cabbages and turnips trying to grow in the fields. Then Turnip Tom had an idea. If only Big Fat Rosie would cry, he would have plenty of water, for when Big Fat Rosie cried she shed such big fat tears that the whole farm became a huge puddle in ten minutes.

He went to look for her and found her sitting on the grass under a big currant bush, drinking fizzy lemonade from a bottle and fanning herself with a duster. The lemonade made small gurgling noises as it went down her wide throat, like this

She looked very, very happy and not in the least bit likely to cry. Tom didn't want to do anything unkind to make her cry, so he sighed again, like this

and went off to comfort the animals.

The next morning, Turnip Tom woke up and listened to Big Fat Rosie snoring her great big snores, like this

He looked out of the window at the shiny blue sky and the dried-up fields and he knew there would be no rain that day. He shook Rosie by the shoulder and she woke up and gave him a big good-morning smile. Turnip Tom knew there would be no tears, either. He sighed, like this

and told Rosie he was going into the village to see if he could find some water for the farm.

"Can I come too?" asked Rosie, putting her feet into fluffy pink slippers.

"Of course," said Turnip Tom.

Harry, the farm-boy, brought the pony and trap round to the door. Annabel, the little brown pony, coughed in a dry, dejected manner, and Harry said, "When pony be coughin', there be water in the offin'."

"What does he mean?" said Rosie, straightening her hat. "Where's the offin'?"

"He means we'll soon have water," said Turnip Tom as he gathered up the reins.

Annabel trotted steadily along to the village, her small hooves daintily missing the stones, like this

CLIP-A-CLOP A-CLIP-A-CLOP CLIP-A-CLOP

They were just slowing down as they entered the village when they heard a lot of shouting. Coming towards them was a crowd of men, all waving banners and shouting something like this

The men were stamping their feet in time with the words, so that it sounded like this

As they came nearer, Turnip Tom and Big Fat Rosie could read the banners and hear the words properly. The men were shouting "More money for bun makers!"

Turnip Tom called to one of the men: "What's it all about?"

The man stopped marching and turned to him.

"It's the cream bun factory," he said. "We've all come out on strike. There'll be no more cream buns until they pay us some more money. More money for bun makers!" Then he went back to the crowd, who were now gathered around their leader at the side of the road, grumbling noisily.

Big Fat Rosie looked at Turnip Tom and said in a little voice, "No more buns?"

Turnip Tom shook his head. "No more buns."

"But I like cream buns more than anything," wailed Big Fat Rosie. "What will I do without my cream buns for breakfast? And lunch? And tea? Oh, this is the most dreadful thing that has ever happened!"

And Big Fat Rosie slumped in her seat and she began to cry, like this

Turnip Tom could hardly stop himself smiling. "There there, dear," he said, and quickly placed his hat on her lap to catch the tears. They were the biggest tears you ever saw and they fell hugely and juicily into the hat, like this

"Come on Annabel!" shouted Turnip Tom to the pony. "We must get back to the farm before she stops crying!" And the pony set off at a fast canter down the lane like this

with Big Fat Rosie still crying, like this

while her tears sprayed out in all directions and Turnip Tom stood up in the cart and shouted with glee.

They soon arrived back at the farm and all the animals hurried round as Rosie stood crying into their drinking trough. Maisie the cow took a long drink. She was so thirsty that she didn't mind about the water being a bit salty. She gave a loud happy moo, like this

and all the hens set up such a cackle you would have thought it was Christmas. One of them sounded like this

and another one like this

Alexander the pig was so happy he was quite speech-less – or rather, gruntless.

When all the animals had had enough water, Turnip Tom led Big Fat Rosie over all the fields. The more she cried, like this

the more the tears fell from her eyes, like this

and everywhere they went, the baby cabbages and turnip tops lifted their heads with bright green smiles. Big Fat Rosie had saved the day!

When they were just finishing the last field, Harry came hurrying over on bent legs.

"News from the village!" he cried. "The cream bun makers have gone back to work! As I always say, when the waterin's done, there'll be cream in the bun."

"There now," said Turnip Tom to Big Fat Rosie, patting her large shoulder, "you can stop crying."

"Owo," said Rosie and stopped short. "Does that mean I can have cream buns for my tea?"

"Yes," said Turnip Tom. "And as you have saved the farm, I will buy you two hundred cream buns for your supper."

"Two hundred!" exclaimed Big Fat Rosie. And she giggled a great big giggle, like this

Ki Ki Ki Ki Ki Ki Ki

and hugged Turnip Tom until he could hardly breathe.

Turnip Tom Makes Hay

IT was time to gather the hay in the big meadow. The long grass had been cut and left to dry in the sun. Now it had to be collected up into a tall stack before the rain could come down and spoil it.

Turnip Tom finished his breakfast and went to the door. It was a lovely day. He sniffed the air, like this

and said to the chickens in the yard: "It's a fine, dry morning. Just right for haymaking." The chickens agreed, like this

CLUCKLE-UCKLE -UCKLE

"Yes," said Turnip Tom. Then he put on his hat and went across the yard to find Harry.

Harry was in the dairy, cleaning the milk churns. He was rinsing them out with a hose, and the water swirled around the churns, making a noise like this

"Come on Harry," cried Turnip Tom. "It's haymaking day."

"Arr," replied Harry. "When the churn's bright and gay, it be time to make hay." He harnessed Lollipop, the big farm horse, to the hay wagon and they all set off for the meadow. When they arrived, they tied Lollipop to the gate and set about raking the hay into piles. Turnip Tom and Harry worked hard, and by the end of the morning the field was covered with large yellow heaps. Turnip Tom mopped his brow with his spotted handkerchief and sighed, like this

He said, "I think it's time for lunch."

Just then they saw Big Fat Rosie coming towards them. She was carrying two large picnic baskets, overflowing with food. Balanced on the top of one of the baskets was a large jug of frothy beer and round Rosie's neck hung a bag of oats for Lollipop.

Lollipop neighed a welcome, like this

"Arr," said Harry. "When farmer's wife comes, there'll be food in our tums."

Turnip Tom propped his rake against the hedge and went to help Big Fat Rosie with the food.

"You're a good wife, Rosie," he said. "You've brought such a lot of food you must have known how hungry I was."

Big Fat Rosie giggled, like this

Ki-Ki-Ki-Ki Ki-Ki-Ki

"I'm having lunch, too," she said. "One of these baskets is full of cream buns."

"Rosie," said Tom, trying to look cross, "you are very, very greedy."

"I know," said Rosie, and they both laughed.

Soon they were all sitting down to their lunch, leaning back lazily against a pile of hay. Turnip Tom said the cold sausage sandwiches were delicious, and Harry, who was very thirsty, drank more than his fair share of the beer. Big Fat Rosie ate twenty-three buns, like this

and got cream all over her chin.

Lollipop got oats all over hers.

When everyone had finished, Turnip Tom stood up.

"Come on, Harry," he said. "We must make a haystack." He lifted his pitchfork on to his shoulder and set off across the meadow. Harry drained the last drop of beer from the jug and followed him.

When they had gone, Rosie put the remains of the picnic into one of the baskets and lay back against the hay. It really was particularly warm weather. Rosie felt very nearly full up with cream buns and very nearly like falling asleep. A bee came out of the hay and buzzed around her, like this

Then a woodpigeon flew out of a nearby tree and sang to her, like this

Big Fat Rosie closed her eyes and felt the sun on her face. The hay was fresh and sweet-smelling, like new sheets. After a very short time, Rosie began to snore – first just a little noise, like this

and then a great big snore, like this

Turnip Tom picked up a large pile of hay on his pitchfork and heaved it on to the wagon. "Gee up, Lollipop," he said. The farm horse began lumbering on her great feet across the meadow, drawing behind her a mountain of rich, golden hay.

Suddenly, a small mouse ran out of the hay and along one of the shafts of the cart. Then it squeaked happily, like this

eeeeek-eeee

– and ran straight down one of Lollipop's front legs!

Poor Lollipop was so surprised and frightened that she reared right up in the air, waving her front feet about like someone learning to swim. The wagon tipped over on its side and all the hay came toppling out. Right on top of Big Fat Rosie.

Turnip Tom and Harry hurried to the scene, and while Tom stroked Lollipop's nose and made calming noises, like this

Harry said "Dearie me," and heaved the cart back on to its wheels.

Buried under the hay, Big Fat Rosie slept on, dreaming about a great big tea table covered with plates of cream buns. She chuckled in her sleep, like this

Tom said to Harry, "This looks like a good enough place to build our haystack," and they began to build the hay up nice and high. The two of them worked all afternoon, throwing heap upon heap of hay on to the pile. Soon the haystack was higher than their heads, but still Big Fat Rosie slept on underneath it.

When all the hay was gathered in, Tom sighed a contented sigh, like this

and told Harry it was time to go home for tea. He looked proudly at the haystack. They had done a fine job and the stack stood tall and gold against the cloudless sky.

"Oi oi oi," said Harry. "Have a listen. Haystack be singing."

"Nonsense," said Turnip Tom. "Haystacks don't sing."

"This one do," said Harry.

Turnip Tom listened and, sure enough, the haystack *was* making a funny noise, like this

"That's not singing," said Turnip Tom. "That's snoring. And I only know one person who snores like that. Big Fat Rosie!"

"Dearie me," said Harry, waggling his head.

"We must get her out," declared Turnip Tom. "Pass me my pitchfork."

He began to lift the hay from the side of the stack, and all of a sudden there was a loud shriek, like this

"What be that?" said Harry.

"Me!" shouted Rosie from under the hay. "Someone stuck a fork in me!"

"Sorry dear," said Turnip Tom and tried again.

"Yowow!" went the haystack. Rosie was so big there was nowhere Tom could stick the fork *without* touching her.

"Oh dear," he said. "If we don't get you out soon, you'll miss your tea."

The haystack began to shake and wobble with loud sobbing noises, like this

Big Fat Rosie was crying.

"Dearie me," said Harry. "Haystack be falling apart."

And it was true. Rosie's big fat tears had made a lake under the haystack and the hay was beginning to float outwards. Soon it was spread all over the field and Rosie was left sitting damply in the middle, still crying, like this

There was hay in her eyes, there was hay in her ears – there was hay all over every bit of her.

"Don't cry," said Turnip Tom. "You haven't missed your tea after all."

"But the hay," sobbed Big Fat Rosie. "It's soaking wet."

"Never mind," said Turnip Tom. "There'll be lots more sunny days and it will all dry out again. There, there, blow your nose." He lent her his spotted handkerchief and she had a good blow, like this

"Next time you go haymaking," said Big Fat Rosie with an extra loud sniff, "I will have my lunch at home. In the kitchen."

The Queen of the Circus

TURNIP Tom and Big Fat Rosie were having breakfast one October morning when they heard a strange noise, like this

It seemed to be coming from the lane.

"Whatever is it?" said Turnip Tom.

"It sounds like an elephant," said Big Fat Rosie.

"Or a lion," said Turnip Tom.

They went to the window and looked out. There, just passing the farm gate, was a long procession of vans and lorries. On the side of one of the vans there were pictures of animals and a sign which said *Signor Ravioli's Grand Circus*. Then came cages of lions and tigers, monkeys, bears and elephants. One of the elephants put out his trunk and tore a piece from Turnip Tom's best hedge. A man in red boots walked past, leading a string of milk-white horses, and a little girl rode on the neck of a camel.

"A circus, a circus!" cried Big Fat Rosie. "Oh please can we go and see it? Please, Turnip Tom!"

"I don't see why not," replied Turnip Tom. "I'll ask Harry if he knows where they are going."

Harry was clearing the autumn leaves from a drainpipe by the cowshed by knocking on the pipe with a hammer, like this

"'Morning Harry," said Turnip Tom. "Did you hear the circus go by?"

"Arr," said Harry. "When there's leaves in your plumbin', the circus be comin'. It be on its way to Farmer Brown's field. Come tomorrow afternoon, they'll be all set up and ready to start, I dare say."

The next day Turnip Tom and Big Fat Rosie set off for the circus. They wore their best clothes and Turnip Tom had a fresh ear of corn in his hat. When they got to Farmer Brown's field they saw a big, striped tent, with a long queue of people waiting to go inside. Standing by the entrance was a clown with a red nose. He shouted to the people in a loud voice like this

Turnip Tom bought two tickets and they went inside. There were rows and rows of seats all facing the big sawdust ring. A band was playing, like this

and a girl in yellow satin was selling programmes
and candy floss.

Turnip Tom bought some candy floss for Big Fat
Rosie and they sat down in the front row and waited
for the circus to begin.

Suddenly, the trumpets blared, like this

45

and into the spotlight walked the Ringmaster. "Good afternoon-a ladies and gentlemen," he bellowed. "I am-a Signor Ravioli. Welcome to my-a wonderful circus, the greatest in the land-a. And to start-a the show, bring on the Grand-a Parade-a!"

Big Fat Rosie clapped loudly and got candy floss all over her dress. There were clowns on stilts, horses with scarlet plumes, acrobats in glittering cloaks, elephants holding each other's tails, dogs jumping through hoops . . . and there was the little girl riding the camel, now dressed in gold from head to toe.

When the Grand Parade was over, the sealions came into the ring and did some funny tricks with big coloured balls. They made a noise like this

and clapped each other politely. Big Fat Rosie thought they were very clever.

Then the clowns came on again and squirted each other with water, which made Turnip Tom laugh so much he almost burst a button on his waistcoat.

After the clowns came Gordoni the acrobat, who stood on his head on the top of a pole, then Samson, the Strong Man, who could pick up a motorbike with his teeth.

When the crowd had finished clapping Samson, Signor Ravioli announced the next act.

"The magnificent-a Caravellis!"

Running into the ring came a troupe of tumblers, all dressed alike in gold shirts and green trousers. They turned cartwheels and leapt in the air, climbed on each other's shoulders and somersaulted off. It was very exciting to watch, especially when the drums rolled like this

and one of the Caravellis did something especially daring. Big Fat Rosie had another mouthful of candy floss and wished she could be a tumbler in green trousers.

Two of the Caravellis fetched a large trampoline and placed it in the middle of the ring. One by one each member of the troupe had his turn on the trampoline, bouncing and turning, going head over heels in space. Then Signor Ravioli came into the ring and made an announcement. "Any member of the audience who would-a like-a to have a go on the trampoline-a may now-a do so."

Before Turnip Tom could stop her, Big Fat Rosie had clambered over the edge of the ring, still clutching her candy floss, and was hurrying towards the trampoline. "Please," she called, "let me have a go!" She was there well before anyone else, but she couldn't climb over the side of the trampoline. She wailed, like this

and six of the Caravellis gave her a shove. She rolled onto the canvas and tried to stand up. It was very difficult, because she kept bouncing about. The audience was laughing and shouting "Jump! Jump!" so Rosie jumped. As she came heavily down onto the trampoline, the springs which held the canvas stretched right down to the ground, then sprang suddenly back. Big Fat Rosie was thrown high into the air. The audience gasped, like this

and cheered when she came down again. The next bounce was even higher and the next one even higher than that. Rosie soared to the top of the tent. This time, however, as she began to come down, Big Fat Rosie fell across the high wire. She hung there, quite out of breath, and everybody stared up at her, open-mouthed. But Big Fat Rosie has always wondered what it would be like to walk along a high wire. She drew herself up and planted her feet on the wire. Then she began to walk along it, wobbling wildly and waving her stick of candy floss. The crowd drew its breath, like this

and then, suddenly, Rosie lost her balance. She toppled off the high wire and fell through the air. Turnip Tom shut his eyes and clutched the side of his seat. Would she fall all the way to the ground?

But Big Fat Rosie was lucky. A trapeze was hanging below the high wire and she managed to grasp it as she fell. She swung this way and that, while the crowd cheered, like this

Big Fat Rosie was quite enjoying herself, way above everyone's heads, but the trapeze was not so happy. The ropes creaked and groaned, like this

as Big Fat Rosie's weight stretched them as far as they could go. All at once there came a tearing sound, and the ropes broke. There was a shocked silence as Rosie dived down into the audience. The candy floss girl had put her tray on the edge of the ring while she watched Big Fat Rosie, and she cried out as the air was suddenly filled with pink, sugary pieces. Big Fat Rosie had landed right in the middle of the candy floss!

Turnip Tom hurried to her. When he saw she was not hurt he gave a sigh of relief, like this

Signor Ravioli wrung his hands in distress. "Poor-a lady," he said. "This is terrible. Are you really all-a right?"

Big Fat Rosie giggled, like this

and said, "Nobody could mind falling into a tray of candy floss." She licked her fingers happily.

"And you were a very good acrobat," said Turnip Tom, pulling her stickily to her feet and getting candy floss on his waistcoat.

Signor Ravioli agreed. "Never has an audience cheered-a as they have cheered-a today. You were the star turn. You are the Queen-a of the Circus!"

The crowd heard him, and roared, like this

and Signor Ravioli told Big Fat Rosie she could have anything she wanted.

"Can I really?" said Big Fat Rosie, her eyes popping out of her head. "Then I should like a new stick of candy floss, please."

"You shall have-a the whole tray," said Signor Ravioli. "And – you shall-a ride-a home-a on my best-a elephant."

And so it was that Big Fat Rosie came to find herself sitting behind Turnip Tom on the back of a big elephant, clutching twenty sticks of candy floss. As they left the circus, she waved to Signor Ravioli and called out, "Can I be Queen of the Circus again? Tomorrow? And the next day? And the day after that?" But the elephant made a noise like this

and Turnip Tom shook his head. Very, very firmly.

Big Fat Rosie's Washday Adventure

IT was a Monday. Big Fat Rosie stood over the kitchen sink, rubbing and scrubbing. First she washed her yellow dress, then her blue skirt, then Turnip Tom's spotted handkerchiefs. She looked out of the kitchen window and saw the wind blowing through the trees. It made a noise like this

Big Fat Rosie could see that it was a good day for drying clothes. She rinsed the soap out of the new pink nightdress that Turnip Tom had given her for her birthday, and she pulled the plug out of the sink. The water ran down the drain, like this

A large iron mangle stood by the back door with a tin tub underneath. Big Fat Rosie used it for squeezing the water out of wet clothes. As she turned the handle, the rollers went round and round, like this

Soon the clothes were ready to hang on the line. Big Fat Rosie carried them out to the garden in a large basket. She held the pegs in her mouth and took them out one by one as she hung out the clothes. First of all she pegged the yellow dress to the line, then the spotted handkerchiefs – and then the nightdress.

At that moment a great gust of wind came whistling through the trees, like this

and tore the nightdress off the line. Filled with air, the nightdress danced about like a balloon, its arms flapping up and down. Big Fat Rosie jumped forward to catch it, but the nightdress flew away as if it were a great bird. Big Fat Rosie cried out, like this

and began to run after it.

The nightdress flipped itself over the garden hedge and made for the fields, with Big Fat Rosie after it. She tore her dress as she scrambled through the hedge, but she didn't even notice. "My birthday present!" she cried. "Come back! Come back here you naughty nightie!"

The nightdress was heading for the duck pond now. Like a ghost it sailed over the water, giving the ducks the fright of their lives. They made a lot of noise, like this

and even more noise when they saw Big Fat Rosie wading through their muddy home as fast as she could manage, like this

Turnip Tom and Harry were in the cowshed when they heard all the splashing and quacking.

"Dearie me," said Harry. "What be the matter?"

They looked towards the duck pond and saw the billowing nightdress chased by a very wet Big Fat Rosie.

"Arr," said Harry. "While we be a-gapin', the nightie's escapin'."

"Quite right," said Turnip Tom. "Come on. After it!"

So they hurried off to the duck pond, with shouts of "To the rescue!" and "Mind the ducklings!" By the time they got there, the nightdress, with Big Fat Rosie only a yard behind, had reached the gate of the field. It lingered for a moment while the wind gathered strength for another blow. Up and down the gate it danced, pretending to jump over. But it waited too long.

"Ha!" shouted Big Fat Rosie. "Got you!" She grabbed the hem of the nightdress and turned round, smiling at the hurrying figures of Harry and Turnip Tom.

Just then, the wind gave another great blow, like this

and the nightdress leapt high over the gate, carrying Big Fat Rosie with it. "Help!" she shouted. "Help! Help-help-help!" But Turnip Tom was too far away to catch her legs and poor old Harry couldn't hurry any faster.

The nightdress carried Big Fat Rosie high over the fields and hedges, its arms stretched out like the wings of an aeroplane. Soon she was quite out of sight of Turnip Tom and heading towards the village.

"We must harness the pony," said Turnip Tom. "We shall go after her."

They headed back to the farmyard and Harry brought his rusty old bicycle out of the feed shed. "I'll take my bike," he said. "It be quicker on the roads." He set off at a fine pace, whizzing through the gateway and out into the lane. "To the village!" he cried. He had not gone more than twenty yards before he heard a noise like this

It was a puncture. Very slowly, the air escaped from the back tyre until there was none left at all. "I mustn't stop," said Harry firmly. "I must get to the village, flat tyre and all." It was very uncomfortable, riding a bicycle with a flat tyre. Apart from the bump, bump as the wheel went round, the bicycle needed oiling. It made a noise like this

Meanwhile, Turnip Tom had harnessed Annabel and was coming up the road behind Harry, like this

He stopped when he saw the flat tyre and offered Harry a lift. But Harry was too proud to leave his bicycle in the ditch and ride in the cart instead, so he went on bumping along while Turnip Tom sped on to the village.

Big Fat Rosie thought she would never reach the ground again. The nightdress had pulled her this way and that, down through thorn bushes, up through oak trees and even round and round a church steeple. She moaned sadly, like this

and wondered if she would ever see dear old Turnip Tom again. Suddenly, the nightdress swept down over the road and began to pull Big Fat Rosie along towards the village. Down below her she could see Turnip Tom in the cart and Harry on his bicycle. "Hallooo!" she shouted, "I'm up here!" But they didn't hear her for the clatter of the pony's hooves and the rattle of Harry's bicycle.

The nightie passed a big house on the edge of the village and Big Fat Rosie looked through the bedroom windows, but there was nobody in. A sports car zoomed past beneath her, like this

but the driver didn't look up. "Oh dear," thought Big Fat Rosie. "Whatever will become of me? If I stay up here much longer I shan't be able to eat. And if I can't eat, I might get quite thin." And she moaned again, like this

Turnip Tom, his face red with excitement, urged the pony to go still faster. The pony snorted, like this

as if to say, "Can't you see my legs are in knots already?"

Harry was wheezing with the effort of pedalling, like this

when he saw in the distance a strange shape in the sky. "It be they!" he croaked to Turnip Tom. "They be floating up the village street."

But however fast Turnip Tom and Harry could go, neither of them could think of a way to get Big Fat Rosie down.

"We could throw a rope up," suggested Turnip Tom, "if we had a rope."

"I could jump very, very high," said Harry, "if I could jump. Which I can't," he added, looking sorrowfully at his bent knees.

So they just stood there and stared as Big Fat Rosie floated away. Turnip Tom sighed, like this

and waited for something to happen. Something *did* happen. Big Fat Rosie and the nightdress flew past the windows of the cream bun factory. Inside, Rosie saw a man squirting cream into the middle of a rich, squashy bun. It made her feel very hungry indeed. "Halloo!" she wailed. The man looked up and was so surprised to see Big Fat Rosie and the big fat nightie that he squirted the cream all over his shoes, like this

He called to the other bun makers to come and see Big Fat Rosie floating by. They gasped and they gaped, horrified to see their best customer being stolen by a nightdress. "We must bring her down," they said to each other. "We must save our champion bun-eater!" They put their heads together and decided there was only one way to save Big Fat Rosie. They must burst the nightie, just like you burst a balloon. But they had no darts, no pins. All they had were cream buns.

"Yowow!" shouted Big Fat Rosie as the first bun hit her. "Yowow!" The bun makers were not very good at throwing, but at last they managed to hit the nightdress. A cream bun landed right in the middle of it, like this

Then another, and another. Slowly, the nightdress bent sideways and became thinner and thinner. And as the nightdress got thinner, it sank lower and lower. At last, Big Fat Rosie reached the ground. She sat down heavily on the pile of cream buns in the village street and the nightdress settled gracefully over her head.

Turnip Tom and Harry came running round the corner.

"There be nightdress," said Harry.

"But where's Rosie?" wondered Turnip Tom.

"Here," said a little voice, and Big Fat Rosie poked her head out from under the nightdress. Then she giggled, like this

Ki-Ki-Ki-Ki-Ki-Ki...

and Turnip Tom hugged her. And when the Manager of the cream bun factory came out to tell Big Fat Rosie that she could take home all the cream buns she could carry in the nightdress, Rosie smiled her biggest smile.

Harry just said, "A journey be fun – if it ends with a bun!"

A Trip to the Town

ONE morning, Turnip Tom came into the kitchen with a strange-looking object in his hand. "Look what I found in Maisie's manger," he said.

Big Fat Rosie took the object from him and peered closely at it. "Do you know what this is?" she asked. "It's my best hat. That cow's been eating my best hat. If it had been my second-best hat I wouldn't mind so much, but this was my very best hat – the one with the cherries." And she put what was left of the hat on her head, sat down heavily on a chair and began to cry, like this

She looked very funny, but Turnip Tom was too kind to laugh at her. Instead, he said, "Let's go into town and buy you a new one. It's a long time since you had a new hat. Cheer up then, my dear, and dry your eyes."

Big Fat Rosie stopped crying with a gulp, like this

and gave Turnip Tom a wide smile. He patted her shoulder and went to tell Harry to harness Annabel, so that they could leave straight away. Big Fat Rosie gave her nose a great blow, like this

and felt much better. She liked going into town.

Harry wanted to go too, so they all climbed into the cart. Turnip Tom took the reins and Big Fat Rosie sat beside him. Harry sat in the back of the cart with his spindly legs dangling over the road.

"With me boots hangin' down," he said, "I be nearer the ground."

Annabel trotted gaily along the road, through the village and on to the big highway that led to the town. Her hooves made a noise like this

and all the people they passed turned to stop and wave.

"They'll wave even harder when we come back," said Turnip Tom to Big Fat Rosie, "because you'll be wearing your smart new hat."

Soon they saw the big buildings of the town ahead of them. There was the station, and the church, and the High Street lined with shops. The pavements were crowded with people going in and out of the shops, bumping into each other and trying to cross the road without being knocked down. A big red car came very close to Annabel and she squealed, like this

and pranced about in the road.

"Whoa there," said Turnip Tom, and decided it was time to park. He tied Annabel's reins to a nearby parking meter and they all jumped down from the cart. "Stay there, Annabel," said Turnip Tom, "we won't be long." Annabel closed her eyes and fell asleep with her chin resting on the boot of the car in front of her.

Big Fat Rosie saw a large shop some way up the street. It looked just the place to buy a new hat. Turnip Tom and Harry wanted to buy some boots, so they told Big Fat Rosie they would meet her outside the shop in half an hour.

When they had gone, Big Fat Rosie looked in the window of the shop. There were lots and lots of hats. She gave a happy giggle, like this

and headed for the revolving doors. But Big Fat
Rosie was too wide for the doors. She got half-way
in and the doors stuck. She pushed and pushed, but
they simply would not move. On the other side a man
made rude faces at her through the glass and waved
his walking stick crossly, but however hard she
pushed, the doors refused to budge. Big Fat Fosie
heaved and heaved, like this

and the rude man hit the doors with his walking stick.
Suddenly, the doors gave way, and Big Fat Rosie shot
forward into the shop like a cork coming out of a
bottle. She landed on her hands and knees and felt
very foolish, but a friendly assistant helped her up
and showed her the way to the hat department.

Big Fat Rosie had never seen so many hats in all her life. There were yellow ones and pink ones, straw hats and felt hats, hats with ribbons, hats with feathers, hats of all shapes and sizes.

She tried on hat after hat and liked all of them. She simply could not make up her mind which one to buy. She was just trying on a blue straw, with daisies round the crown, when she had a dreadful thought and gasped, like this

Turnip Tom had forgotten to put any money in the parking meter! If the traffic warden came along, he might give Annabel a parking ticket or, worse still, arrange for her to be towed away. Poor Annabel!

Big Fat Rosie hurried down the stairs as fast as she could go and made for the shop door. She wasn't going to get stuck in the revolving doors again, so she went out of the big side door and began to run towards Annabel. Then she felt a heavy hand on her arm and a stern voice said, "And where do you think you're going?"

"To save Annabel," puffed Big Fat Rosie, quite out of breath.

"I must ask you to come with me," said the man. "I am the store detective and I have reason to believe you are in possession of goods which have not been paid for."

"What do you mean?" asked Big Fat Rosie.

The man coughed, like this

"Madam," he said. "You have stolen a hat."

All too late, **Big Fat Rosie** realised what she had done. She had been in such a hurry to get to the parking meter that she had quite forgotten to take off the hat with the daisies. It was still on her head.

"B-b-but I didn't mean to," she stammered. "I would have come back."

"You'll still have to come and see the Manager," said the store detective.

Just then, Turnip Tom and Harry came round the corner, wearing their shiny new boots. "What be up?" said Harry. "What's happening?" said Turnip Tom. So Big Fat Rosie explained.

The store detective said, "I think you'd *all* better see the Manager," and took them into the shop.

The Manager sat behind his desk in a large office, smoking a fat cigar and adding up lists of figures. When he had heard what the store detective had to say, he looked very solemn. "We had better call the police," he said. "This lady was obviously trying to steal that hat."

Now, Turnip Tom could not stand by while someone called his wife a shoplifter. He made a cross noise, like this

and went towards the Manager with his fists raised. Harry stood behind him, trying to look extremely fierce.

The Manager put his cigar in the ash tray and stood up. "Now, now," he said, "I will not have violence in my office. Jenkins," he turned to the store detective, "fetch the police."

It was all too much for Big Fat Rosie and she began to cry. Her shoulders shook and wobbled and she made a noise like this

"Just a moment," said the Manager, sniffing the air. "I can smell burning." A thin column of smoke was rising from the side of his desk.

"Waste-paper basket be on fire," said Harry, nodding his head. "That cigar be so fat and round it rolled off your desk."

"Help!" shouted the Manager, shivering like a pale jelly. "Fire! Fire!"

But Turnip Tom knew just what to do. Big Fat Rosie was still crying, and when Big Fat Rosie cried, there was enough water to put out ten fires. Already the tears were lapping at the soles of his new boots.

"Over here," he said as he steered Big Fat Rosie towards the waste-paper basket. "A couple of tears will do it."

Big Fat Rosie's tears fell perlop-perlap-sperlish-sperlash over the carpet. "This way a bit," said Turnip Tom. Two fat tears dropped into the flaming waste-paper, putting the fire right out, like this

"I say," said the Manager. "Well done! You've saved us all. The whole shop might have gone up in flames."

"Arr," said Harry.

"What are you going to do about my wife?" demanded Turnip Tom. "If she cries for much longer we might all be drowned."

"She shall have the best hat in the shop," said the Manager. "No, she shall have all the hats she wants. She can have a hundred hats!"

Big Fat Rosie almost stopped crying.

"And do you still say I'm a shoplifter?" she sniffed.

"Of course not," said the Manager, looking very guilty. "Come this way and choose your hats."

Outside in the street, Annabel was a bit fed up with waiting. When a traffic warden had come to check her meter she had bared her teeth at him and he had moved quickly on. Since then, nothing had happened. She blew through her nose, like this

and settled down for another nap. But before she knew where she was there were shouts and laughs and the cart was being filled with hats: big hats, small hats, spring hats, summer hats, sun hats and rain hats. And there was Big Fat Rosie climbing up to her seat wearing four hats at once, one on top of the other. "They're all mad," thought Annabel, "quite mad."

"And one for you," the Manager was saying, and he placed on Annabel's head a floppy straw hat with holes cut in it for her ears.

"There," said Turnip Tom. "You're the smartest pony in town."

"I'll remember this day," nodded Harry, "till me hair be turned grey." This was odd, because Harry's hair was grey already. But with his new purple tam o'shanter pulled firmly down over his ears, he didn't think anyone would notice.

The Great Toboggan Race

Big Fat Rosie was sure it was going to snow. "See how heavy the sky is," she said, looking out of the kitchen window as she dried up the breakfast plates.

Turnip Tom opened the back door and kicked at the ice on the boot-scraper. "I'd better keep the cows in," he said.

Then Harry came hurrying across the yard, banging his arms against his body to keep warm. His frozen breath hung around his head like the steam from a kettle. "'Mornin' Mister Tom," he began, then he stepped on a patch of ice and his feet went flying out from under him. He let out a yell, like this

and landed thump on his back. He sat up slowly, rubbing his bruises, then he looked at the sky and declared: "When your boots go astray, there be snow on the way."

And he was quite right. Just before lunch, the snow began to fall. It spattered against the window panes and settled snugly on the henhouse roof. The chickens inside clucked contentedly, like this

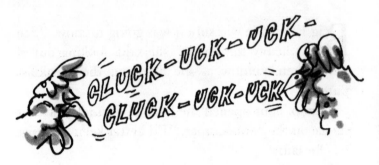

and settled down for a nap. Alexander the pig stuck his head through the door of his sty and felt the sting of cold snowflakes on his pink nose. He grunted happily, like this

and put out his tongue to see how they tasted.

By tea-time the farm was several inches deep in soft, fluffy snow. Big Fat Rosie toasted some muffins and put an extra log on the fire. She opened the back door to shout "Tea-ea!" and Turnip Tom came hurrying in, shaking the snow from his hat.

Big Fat Rosie giggled, like this

Ki-Ki-Ki-Ki-Ki-Ki-Ki

and said he looked like a walking ice-cream.

They ate their tea by the fire, keeping the muffins warm on the hearth, and Turnip Tom said he thought it would snow for several days.

"Wop fum!" said Big Fat Rosie, her mouth full of muffin. "Shall we skape on the duck pom?"

"No," answered Turnip Tom. "You would be sure to fall through the ice."

"Then can I make a slide in the yard?"

"That's very dangerous. The cows might fall over on their way to be milked."

"Then can we go tobogganing down Hawthorn Hill?"

"We haven't got a toboggan."

Big Fat Rosie offered him another muffin. "You could make one, couldn't you?" she pleaded.

"Yes," said Turnip Tom. "I could."

So that evening he went out to the barn with his saw and hammer. Big Fat Rosie could hear toboggan-making noises ringing through the night air, like this

While Turnip Tom sawed and hammered, Big Fat Rosie took out her knitting needles and began to make woolly hats and scarves. Turnip Tom's would be green and hers would be yellow. How smart they would look as they rode their toboggan.

She sat in her big rocking chair and knitted steadily, her needles flashing in the firelight, like this

Soon, she thought happily, we will be whizzing down
Hawthorn Hill, faster and faster and faster and
faster . . .

In two days, her knitting was finished. She had run
out of yellow wool half-way through making her own
hat, and it sat on the top of her bouncy curls like a
tea-cosy. Turnip Tom wound his green scarf around
his neck and went to fetch his toboggan from the shed.
Its scarlet runners slid smoothly across the yard to the
back door.

"Beautiful!" cried Big Fat Rosie, clapping her
hands together.

Turnip Tom coughed modestly, like this

HEM HEM!

and said, "I'm glad you think so."

Together they set off for Hawthorn Hill, pulling the toboggan between them. Their rubber boots made deep holes in the snow and marked their trail over the white fields. When they reached the top of Hawthorn Hill, they saw a crowd of children gathered there, all of them wearing woolly hats and some of them pulling bright toboggans.

One of the children was crying, like this

"It's Billy Perkins from the village," said Big Fat Rosie. "What's the matter, Billy?"

"It's my brother Bert," sobbed Billy. "He says I'm too young to ride on his toboggan."

Bert Perkins thrust his hands into his pockets and shrugged his shoulders. "He slows it down with his feet," Bert complained.

Turnip Tom sighed, like this

and took Billy's hand. "Come along," he said. "You can ride with us. And," he added, "I bet we'll be the fastest toboggan of all."

"A race! A race!" shouted the children. "Let's have a race!"

"Very well," said Turnip Tom, "a race it is." And he sat down on his toboggan. Big Fat Rosie sat behind and Billy perched on the back, clinging like a monkey. When everyone was ready, Bert Perkins shouted "Ready, steady, go!" and Turnip Tom pushed away with his feet. The toboggan took off, its runners slicing cleanly through the snow. The wind rushed past and Big Fat Rosie shouted out, like this

She was having the time of her life.

They were going much faster than the others, because they were far, far heavier than the children and their weight carried them along at a colossal speed. Little Billy Perkins had never been so fast. His eyes were as shiny as his pink cheeks as he looked round to see where the others had got to. They were going *much* too slowly to catch up, and Bert Perkins looked rather cross.

As they sped towards the bottom of the hill, Turnip Tom could see ahead of them a great pile of snow which had drifted against a hedge. When they were almost on top of it, he tried to stop.

"Whoa there!" he shouted, as if the toboggan were a horse. He pulled on the rope and dug his boots into the snow, but still they rushed forward.

Billy Perkins cried out in fright, like this

and Big Fat Rosie held tight to Turnip Tom's back. It was no use. They were not going to pull up in time.

When the other toboggans reached the foot of the hill, the children looked around. Turnip Tom, Big Fat Rosie and Billy Perkins were nowhere to be seen. On its side, leaning against the snowdrift, was the big toboggan, and perched on the end of one of the runners was Big Fat Rosie's yellow hat.

"Where can they be? Where's our Billy?" asked Bert Perkins, sorry now that he had been unkind to his brother.

There was a flurry of snow, and Billy jumped out of the snowdrift, waving his arms. "We couldn't stop," he explained. "We got buried."

The children gathered round to dig Big Fat Rosie and Turnip Tom out of the snowdrift. First of all they found Turnip Tom's green scarf, then his green hat, then Turnip Tom himself. His teeth were chattering from the cold, like this

UN-UN-UN...

Then, right at the bottom, they found Big Fat
Rosie. All together, they heaved her out and she sat
heavily in the snow, crying like this

"What's up, Rosie?" asked Turnip Tom, putting his arm around her.

"I'm ker-ker-ker-ker," she stuttered.

"You're what?"

"I'm ker-ker-ker-ker-"

"I think she's cold," said Billy Perkins. "Let's wrap her up with our scarves and take her home."

So they all set off for the farm. Four of the bigger boys helped Turnip Tom to pull Big Fat Rosie on her toboggan. Billy Perkins pushed from behind. Big Fat Rosie, wrapped up like a Christmas present in coloured scarves, giggled, like this

She thought it was a lovely way to travel.

"You must all come in for tea," she announced.

Harry met them at the gate and they told him what had happened. "Dearie me," he exclaimed anxiously.

"But we won the race," said Rosie, smiling proudly.

"Arr then," said Harry, "when a race has been won, the – er, the prize is a bun!"

"Cream buns!" cried Big Fat Rosie, leaping up from the toboggan and tripping over her scarves. "Everyone into the kitchen for tea and buns!"

They trooped inside and had the largest tea of their lives. Big Fat Rosie ate more buns than anyone else, like this

because, she explained, "The more buns I eat, the heavier I'll become. And the heavier I get, the faster the toboggan will go, and the faster the toboggan goes, the more races we'll win, and the more races we win, the more buns I can eat." She laughed. "Do you know," she said, "I could eat a million buns!"

"If you did that," said Turnip Tom, "you'd be so heavy you'd break the toboggan. Then where would we be?"

"I expect," said Big Fat Rosie, "we'd be in the snow."